GRAMMAR RAY
A Graphic Guide to Grammar
PUNCTUATION AND SENTENCES

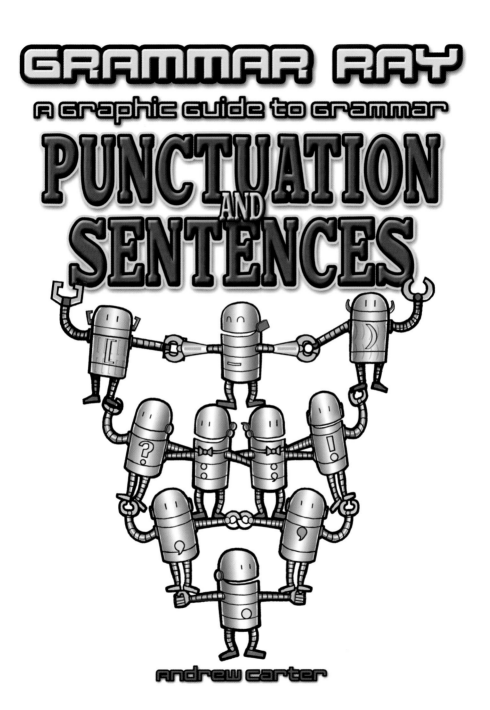

andrew carter

alphabet
s o u p
an imprint of
WINDMILL BOOKS
New York

Published in 2010 by Windmill Books, LLC
303 Park Avenue South, Suite # 1280, New York, NY 10010-3657

Published by Evans Brothers Limited
2A Portman Mansions
Chiltern Street
London W1U 6NR
© in this edition Evans Brothers Limited 2010
© in the text and illustration Andrew Carter 2010

Adaptations to North American Edition © 2010 Windmill Books

CREDITS:
Written by: Andrew Carter
Editor: Bryony Jones
Designer: Mark Holt

Library of Congress Cataloging-in-Publication Data

Carter, Andrew, 1979-
Punctuation and sentences / Andrew Carter. -- North American ed.
p. cm. -- (Grammar ray: a graphic guide to grammar)
ISBN 978-1-60754-740-2 (lib. bdg.) -- ISBN 978-1-60754-751-8 (pbk.) --
ISBN 978-1-60754-752-5 (6-pack)
1. English language--Punctuation--Juvenile literature. 2. English language--Sentences--Juvenile literature.
3. English language--Grammar--Juvenile literature. I. Title.
PE1450.C38 2010
428.2--dc22
2009041409

CPSIA Compliance Information: Batch #EW0102W: For further information contact Windmill Books, New York, New York at 1-866-478-0556.

Manufactured in China

contents

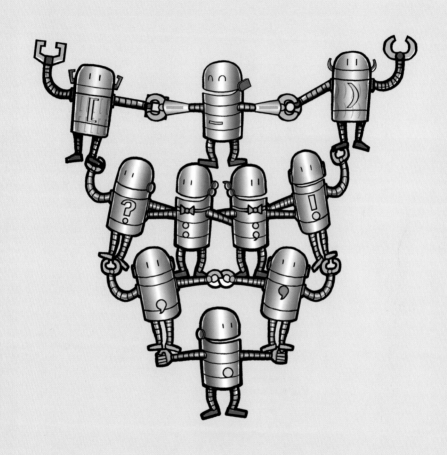

INTRODUCTION

Hello and welcome to Grammar Ray!
English grammar comes to life in this world of
fun and adventure. Words in the English language are
divided into groups called "parts of speech." This book
will introduce you to a group of robots on a quest to
discover how the parts of speech fit together
to make sentences.

We are the punctuation robots.
Follow us to learn how we make the world
of written English make sense!

The first part of the book is a comic strip.
The robots will demonstrate how the different
punctuation marks work and will use some
super-strong conjunctions as the glue that
joins the parts of a sentence together.

Following the robots' adventures,
the rest of the book explores sentence
construction in more detail. Use the examples
in this section if you need a reminder of the role
punctuation and sentences play in English
grammar. Don't forget your puzzle-solving
skills, because you will be tested on what you
have learned along the way. So be sure
to pay attention!

Before we look at punctuation and sentences, let's start right at the beginning and look at the basics of written English.

In English there are 26 letters in the alphabet.

We combine letters to make words.

words

Every word in English is a *part of speech.* Let's take a look at the most common parts of speech.

Nouns name things e.g. *cat, family, Tokyo, love*

Pronouns can replace nouns e.g. *he, she, they, this*

Adjectives describe nouns e.g. *big, happy, green, many*

Verbs describe physical or mental actions e.g. *jump, play, think, be*

Adverbs describe how something is done e.g. *quickly, well, sadly*

Prepositions tell us about position and movement e.g. *on, at, up*

We combine these parts of speech to make *sentences.*

Conjunctions are the words that join words, phrases, and parts of sentences.

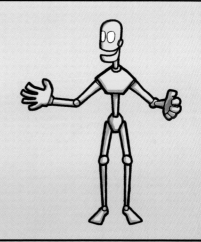

So what are punctuation marks?

Punctuation marks are the small symbols that we use to give meaning to sentences and help them to make sense.

Here is a handful of the most common.

Now let's take a look at them individually and see how they can be used...

8

1. The period

Periods are most commonly used to end a sentence:

The robot was hungry.

We also use periods in abbreviations:

P.S.   J.K. Rowling   P.M.

Abbreviated titles for people need a period at the end:

Mr. Dr. Mrs.

2. The exclamation mark

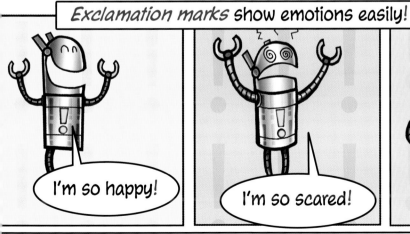

An exclamation mark can be used to add emphasis or expression.

Help!   Don't eat all the pizza!   This is great!

3. The question mark

We use a question mark at the end of a sentence to make it clear that we are asking a question. If we use a question mark we do not need to use a period:

How long is a piece of string?

Why did the chicken cross the road?

4. Parentheses and Brackets

Parentheses are great at carrying extra information [and so are their cousins, brackets.]

Parentheses can contain words that could be taken out of a sentence without changing its meaning, but that carry extra information:

The rabbit *(who was getting hungry now)* jumped through the grass.

Brackets are used to add words that clarify or explain the meaning of a sentence without giving extra information:

She looked up at the hero *[Verb-Man]* as he flew across the sky.

5. The comma

Commas are good at breaking up sentences.

We use a comma to break up a sentence and give a short pause within it.

Although it was tiny, the caterpillar ate a huge leaf by itself.

The dog, who was barking noisily, chased after its own tail.

A comma is also used to separate adjectives in a sentence.

A giant, black, evil monster towered over the scared villagers.

Another use for commas is to separate items in a list.

The magician reached into his hat and pulled out a white rabbit, a small monkey, a can of soda, and a packet of seeds.

Also use a comma when you address somebody by their name.

Hello, Verb-Man!

Show us a trick, Magnificent Pronoun!

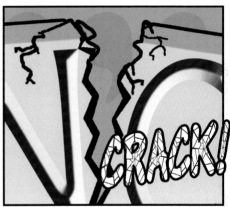

11

6. The apostrophe

Apostrophes are very good at two particular tasks.

1. They can be used to show that one or more letters are missing.

it's = it is   don't = do not   I'll = I will

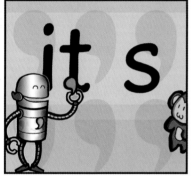

2. Used with an "s" they can tell us that something belongs to someone.

7. The colon

Colons are very good at introducing lists.

 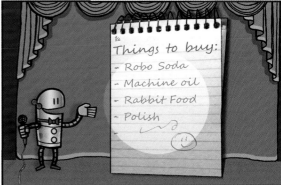

We can use colons to introduce a list or bullet points.

He describes himself with three words: cool, handsome, and modest.

Punctuation marks that we use to end a sentence:

- *Period*
- *Question mark*
- *Exclamation mark*

We also use them to join two statements when the second statement explains the first one.

The Incredible Noun performed tricks: he explained what nouns were.

The man transformed into his alter ego: he became Verb-Man.

Colons are also used to introduce a quotation.

The clown whispered to the ringmaster: "Does my hair look funny?"

8. Quotation marks

Quotation marks are very useful to repeat other people's words.

When we want to show that something has been said by someone, we can use *quotation marks*. There are double (" ") and single (' ') marks, and single marks go inside double marks.

"I'm rather hungry," the greedy cat grumbled aloud to himself.
"He shouted 'Hooray' and left," said Sally.

When you write direct speech, remember the following things:
Always start a new line when a new person starts speaking.

"Who's that?" asked the boy.
"That's Verb-Man!" answered his friend.

Before you close or re-open quotation marks, include punctuation.

"Yes," he said, "I am Verb-Man."
"Woof!" barked the dog.
She asked, "Where?"

You should also use *quotation marks* to show that text has come from another written source such as a book or magazine and also for song titles.

Gazing up at the night sky he hummed
"Twinkle, Twinkle, Little Star."

9. The hyphen

Hyphens are great at connecting things.

Hyphens have several uses:

1. They can join certain words and numbers together.

   T-shirt   forty-two   vice-president

2. They can link words to create compound adjectives.

   A red, bearded robot = a red robot with a beard.

By adding a hyphen you can change the meaning.

A red-bearded robot = a robot with a red beard.

3. They can connect one part of a word to the other if it is split across two lines.

   Verb-Man flew into the sky, his jets streak-
   ing behind him. Far below the rescued vil-
   lagers waved and cheered.

10. The semicolon

Semicolons create longer pauses than commas.

Use a semicolon to link two sentences without using a word like "and" or "but":

He opened the box; there was a strange glow inside.
The robot was thirsty; he bought a drink.

Semicolons can also be used like commas to separate things in a list:

In the box he found: a hat; a wand; a bow tie and a rabbit.

11. The ellipsis

Ellipses like to build suspense.

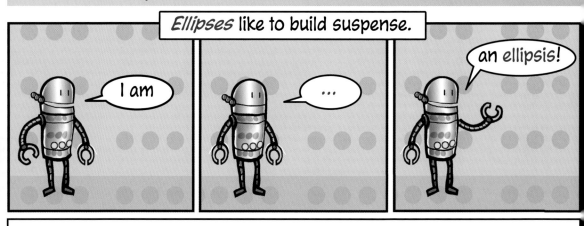

An *ellipsis* can be used to end a sentence to suggest that words have deliberately been left out, so it is often used to build suspense, e.g.

She would only have one bullet to stop the monster:
she aimed her pistol, pulled the trigger and...

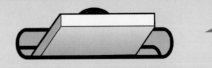

CONJUNCTIONS GLUE

Extra Strength ✓

Long Lasting ✓

Rapidly bonds parts of speech ✓

UNIQUE NEW FORMULA

Sticks nouns, verbs, adverbs pronouns, prepositions, and adjectives!

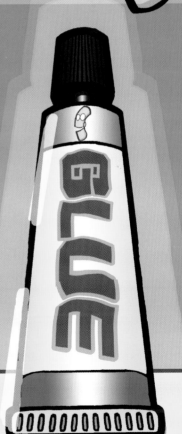

Net Weight 4oz

Net Weight 4oz

Net Weight 4oz

Conjunctions are the words that we use to join words, phrases, and parts of sentences.

Did you know that conjunctions are often also called connectives?

Here are some of the most common conjunctions:

although

and

as

but

since

because

Let's take a look at how conjunctions are used in some sentences.

CONJUNCTIONS
GLUE

Instructions *for* use:

Ensure that any parts of speech are clean and free of any dirt, dust, or grease, but make sure they are not wet. Apply Conjunctions Glue to a word, phrase or part of a sentence and connect it to another. Hold firmly together for a few seconds to form an initial bond, leave for a further 10 minutes to enable the glue to dry completely.

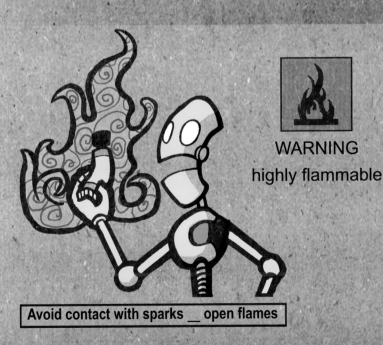

WARNING

highly flammable

WARNING

do not touch

Made in the U.S.A.

4 oz

Avoid contact with sparks __ open flames

1 0271X0 157803

sentences

**A sentence is made up of different parts of speech.
You use them like building blocks to make a complete sentence.**

Let's start the sentence with a noun (**fox**) and an article (the).

The fox is the main focus of the sentence so it becomes known as the "*subject*." The subject usually comes first in a sentence.

FOR EXAMPLE:

The *fox*

Now add a verb (**jumps**) after the subject to explain what the fox is doing.

Now that we have a subject and a verb we have a complete sentence.

FOR EXAMPLE:

The *fox jumps.*

Many sentences contain more than just a subject and a verb. They usually contain an "*object*" too. An object is a noun that is having the verb of the sentence done to it. So in this sentence the **dog** is the object. It is being jumped over.

Of course, we need to add an article (the) to the noun (**dog**) so that the sentence makes sense.

Finally we can add a preposition (over) to explain the fox's movement further.

This sentence now contains a subject (The fox), a verb (jumps), a preposition (over) and an object (the dog).

FOR EXAMPLE:

The fox jumps over **the** dog.

Many sentences contain more than just a subject, verb and object. Finally we can add more information about the fox and the dog by adding some adjectives (brown, lazy and gray). We can add an adverb (quickly) to describe how the fox jumped.

FOR EXAMPLE:

The brown fox jumps quickly over **the** lazy, gray dog.

The final sentence is called a *pangram* because it contains all the letters of the alphabet. Can you spot them all?

PUNCTUATION AND SENTENCES
Test Yourself

Don't write in your Grammar Ray book. Please use a separate sheet of paper to test yourself!

1. What is the name of each punctuation mark?

(a) ?   (b) ;   (c) " "   (d) '   (e) -

2. Which conjunction best completes the sentence?

The robot was glad that his new arms had arrived,
_ _ _ _ _ _ _ he felt there might have been some mistake.

(a) because

(b) since

(c) however

(d) or

REPLAC
ARI

3. Arrange the words into a sentence.

vegetarian The drank juice vampire the thirstily tomato.

Turn the page upside down to see the answers!

1. (a) question mark (b) semicolon (c) quotation marks (d) apostrophe (e) hyphen. 2. however. 3. The vegetarian vampire drank the tomato juice thirstily

GLOSSARY

conjunction (cun-JUNK-shun) a word that connects two other words to each other

exclamation mark (ek-skluh-MAY-shun mark) a punctuation mark used to show high emotion like excitement or anger

flammable (FLA-muh-bull) something that easily catches on fire

pangram (PAN-grum) a sentence that uses all 26 letters of the alphabet

parentheses (pah-REN-thuh-sees) curved punctuation marks that can be put in a sentence to add information without changing the meaning

punctuation (punk-chew-WAY-shun) standard marks that separate words into sentences

symbols (SIM-bowlz) something that represents something else

vegetarian (veh-jeh-TARY-un) someone who does not eat meat

INDEX